Kitty Cat in the Jungle

Written and Illustrated by Leslie Greiner

Kitty Cat in the Jungle

Copyright © 2023 by Leslie Greiner
ISBN 978-1-960007-00-1

Published by
Little Blessing Books
an imprint of
Orison Publishers, Inc.
PO Box 188, Grantham, PA 17027
www.OrisonPublishers.com

"You must be adaptable. Just like the leaves swaying in the wind, you need to flow with the jungle ways. Be curious and open to what life brings your way," said the frog.

"Travel along and my jungle friends will help you find your sense of belonging."

Kitty Cat tiptoed along, trying to sense the jungle ways.

Kitty Cat stumbled upon a leaf-cutter ant.

"Excuse me, Leaf-cutter Ant. What can I do to feel like I belong in the jungle?"

"You can learn to work in harmony with yourself and your jungle friends. Let me hear the strength of your roar."

Kitty Cat let out a very timid roar. "Rrrrrr…"

"Keep wandering along. Your strength will come."

Kitty Cat was wandering along, practicing his roar, when he spotted a blue morpho butterfly soaring among the jungle trees.

"Excuse me, Blue Morpho Butterfly. What can I do to feel like I belong in the jungle?"

"Allow your wings to spread and keep faith in yourself."

Kitty Cat came upon a sloth moving very slowly above him.

"Excuse me, Sloth. What should I do to feel like I belong in the jungle?"

"Slow down and relax. Be present here, in this moment. Breathe in the air and soak in all the beauty around you. Then you will feel like you belong."

Kitty Cat took a deep breath, and as he exhaled, he did feel as if he were part of the beautiful jungle.

Kitty Cat spread his imaginary wings, shimmied along and strengthened his roar even more...

"RRROOoa."

Camouflaged in the vines of the jungle, an iguana moved, catching Kitty Cat's eye.

"Excuse me, Iguana. What should I do to feel like I belong in the jungle?"

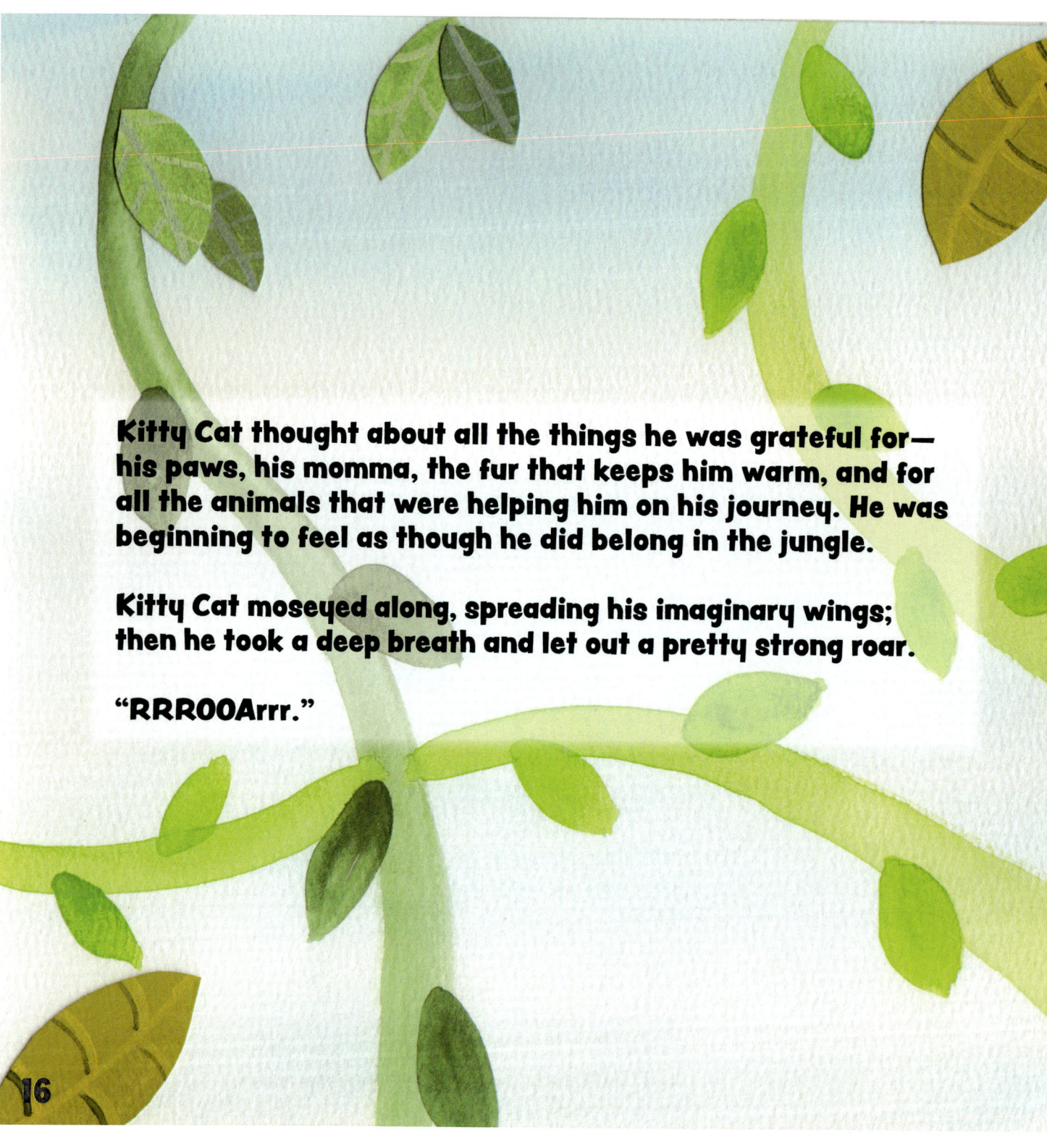

Kitty Cat thought about all the things he was grateful for—his paws, his momma, the fur that keeps him warm, and for all the animals that were helping him on his journey. He was beginning to feel as though he did belong in the jungle.

Kitty Cat moseyed along, spreading his imaginary wings; then he took a deep breath and let out a pretty strong roar.

"RRROOArrr."

Suddenly, a mango dropped from the trees.
And there above him was a monkey.

"Stop being so serious, Kitty Cat. Bring your playful heart to those around you. When you share your playful heart, the world will smile back at you, and you will feel that you belong."

Kitty Cat stood tall, spread his imaginary wings, took a deep breath, and followed the vines with his grateful, playful heart. And then he led out a roar that shook the branches.

"RRROOOARRrrr!"

A toucan squawked above him.

"Excuse me, Toucan; can you tell me how to feel as though I belong in the jungle?"

"You must face your fears. With strength and confidence, you will feel like you belong in the jungle."

Kitty Cat pondered that advice. He did fear that because he was so much smaller than other jungle cats, no one would hear him or listen to him. As Kitty Cat pranced along, he flapped his imaginary wings, took a deep breath, and, leading with his grateful and playful heart, he tried again.

"RRROOOARRRRr!"

"That's a pretty good roar you have," said a jaguar from behind the jungle leaves.

"Excuse me, Jaguar. How can I fit in, here in the jungle?"

"Kitty Cat, you must always speak your truth," said the jaguar. "Share your wisdom with the world. By being your kitty-cat self, you will belong in the jungle."

And with that mighty roar, all of the jungle animals came to his side.

"You are loved, Kitty Cat, and you belong in the jungle," the jaguar said. "You just had to discover who you are and find your strength."